Fantastic Folk Tales

THE MAGIC PAINTBRUSH

Chinese Folk Tale

Om Books International

Ma Liang was a kind and poor man, who lived in a small village in China. He looked after an old man's cattle in his village; but one thing which he loved to do most was to paint. He would paint anywhere and anytime, all the time.

One night, he saw a very strange dream. He saw an old wise man who said, "My dear boy, I am gifting you this magic paintbrush. Use it to help the poor people." So saying, the wise old man vanished.

When Ma Liang awoke the next morning, he was quite surprised to see the magic paintbrush on his table.

Later, on his way to the old man's house, he met some troubled farmers. He asked them, "Why do you look so troubled?" One of them replied, "The river has dried up. We do not have water to drink or irrigate our farms. It is terrible!"

Just then an idea struck Ma Liang. He started painting water on the dried river bed. The farmers heard a loud rumbling noise just as Ma Liang finished his painting. They screamed with joy as they saw Ma Liang's painting come to life. The dried river bed was filled with clear, blue water!

Ma Liang continued to help the poor with his magic paintbrush, and soon the news of the miracles spread through the land, far and wide. Now, there was an evil rich man in the village who got to know about the magic paintbrush. He decided to steal the magic paintbrush to become even richer than he was!

He hired men to steal the magic paintbrush from Ma Liang. As soon as that was in his possession, he called his family and friends over to his house for a treat!

The evil rich man started drawing pots of gold on a paper with the magic paintbrush. But alas, nothing that he drew came to life! The evil man was very angry and he ordered his soldiers to bring Ma Liang before him.

When Ma Liang arrived, the old man told him, “I will give you a good offer. You will draw whatever I desire and I shall let you go.” Ma Liang didn’t want to help the evil rich man, but suddenly he had an idea. He bowed and replied, “I will surely help you.”

The evil rich man excitedly ordered Ma Liang, “Quick, paint me a golden mountain. I will gather the gold and become even richer!” Ma Liang painted a sea, which immediately came to life. The evil rich man was not happy and he screamed, “Why did you paint a sea? I asked you to paint me a golden mountain!”

Ma Liang drew the golden mountain he was asked to draw in the middle of the sea. The evil rich man could not hide his joy and screamed happily, "Quick! Paint me a ship so that I can cross the sea and go to my mountain at once."

The ship that Ma Liang painted, came to life and the evil rich man and his friends immediately went aboard to go to the golden mountain. As soon as they reached the middle of the sea, Ma Liang drew a giant wave. The evil rich man and his greedy friends were swept away by the wave which took them far, far away from China.

As soon as the evil rich man was gone, Ma Liang was a free man. By now, the story of the magic paintbrush had spread like wildfire through all of China and as always, Ma Liang always used his magic paintbrush to help the poor in their times of need.